The Birthday Bear

By Antonie Schneider

Illustrated by Uli Waas

Translated by J. Alison James

North-South Books

NEW YORK · LONDON

For Mimi, Anna and Josi   A.S.

Copyright © 1996 by Nord-Süd Verlag AG, Gossau Zürich, Switzerland.
First published in Switzerland under the title *Der geburtstags-bär*.
English translation copyright © 1996 by North-South Books Inc.

First published in the United States, Great Britain, Canada,
Australia, and New Zealand in 1996 by North-South Books,
an imprint of Nord-Süd Verlag AG, Gossau Zürich, Switzerland.
First paperback edition published in 1998 by North-South Books.

Library of Congress Cataloging-in-Publication Data
Schneider, Antonie.
[Geburtstags-bär. English]
The birthday bear / by Antonie Schneider ;
illustrated by Uli Waas ; translated by J. Alison James.
Summary: David and his sister Sally get a surprise visitor
when they celebrate his birthday in the country with Grandma and Grandpa.
[1. Grandparents—Fiction. 2. Birthdays—Fiction. 3. Bears—Fiction.]
I. Waas, Uli, ill. II. James, J. Alison. III. Title.
PZ7.S3617Bi 1991 [E]—dc20 96-21747

A CIP catalogue record for this book is available from The British Library.

ISBN 1-55858-655-5 (TRADE BINDING)
1 3 5 7 9 TB 10 8 6 4 2
ISBN 1-55858-656-3 (LIBRARY BINDING)
1 3 5 7 9 LB 10 8 6 4 2
ISBN 1-55858-994-5 (PAPERBACK)
1 3 5 7 9 PB 10 8 6 4 2

Printed in Belgium

For more information about our books, and the authors and artists
who create them, visit our web site: http://www.northsouth.com

A NORTH-SOUTH PAPERBACK

Critical praise for

The Birthday Bear

"This book has cheery illustrations that are nicely done. It is an excellent story that ties in birthdays, grandparents, multiculturalism, and how reading can take you away into other worlds."

An *American Bookseller* "Pick of the Lists"

"This short story revolves around David and Sally's trip to the mountains, where they visit their grandparents. In a throwback to old-fashioned living, Grandpa makes fishing rods for the children in his workshop while Granny sets up a tent and bakes a birthday cake for David. . . . Tension arises when a bear comes into camp and eats David's cake. . . . A light, easy-going tale for early readers."

School Library Journal

Every summer David and his older
sister Sally visit their grandparents in
the country. They live where there are
mountains and rivers, old forests—
and bears!

This year Sally and David arrived on David's seventh birthday.

"Granny," said David, "for my birthday I want a big cake, and I want to spend the night in the tent and go fishing with Grandpa."

"Certainly," said Granny.

Granny's house was on a hill at the foot of the mountains. It was built entirely out of wood. Behind the house Grandpa had his workshop. But most of the time he sat down by the river and fished.

When the children saw him, they ran down the hill to the water, shouting, "Grandpa, will you make us fishing rods?"

Then Grandpa went whistling up the hill to his workshop and made a pair of fishing rods.

And Sally and David ran right back
down to the river.

Later Sally and Granny put up the tent. David wasn't allowed to help because it was his birthday treat. So he just lay back in the noonday sun and watched.

That afternoon Sally and David played
on the bank of the big river.

Grandpa came down the river road on his bike.

"Hello, children!" he called.

With a loud war whoop David burst out of the bushes.

Grandpa had to brake sharply.

"Don't move!" cried David, and he swung his tomahawk. "Indian territory!"

"Oh, I see," said Grandpa. "You're right, you know. All the land around here used to belong to the Blackfoot Indians."

"Are there any Indians now?" asked
David.

"Sure," said Grandpa.

"And do they wear headbands with
feathers like ours?"

"Some tribes wore headbands with
feathers a long time ago," said Grandpa.
"Now most Indians dress just like you
and me."

"For my birthday let's all wear feathers
like those long-ago Indians," said David.

"Okay," agreed Grandpa. He took a piece
of fishing line, tied it around his head, and
stuck in a duck feather. "How do I look?"

"Great!" said David.

Grandpa got back on his bicycle and
waved good-bye.

David and Sally ran back to the tent.
Granny was busy decorating the cake.

Suddenly David remembered the Indian
book that he'd been reading. He tried to
recall what had been happening last. . . .
The Indian boy, Little Crow, had his camp
set up on the riverbank, when suddenly a
bear . . .

"Granny, Granny!" cried David. "Have you seen the book about Little Crow?"

"No, my dear. Where were you reading it last?" Granny replied.

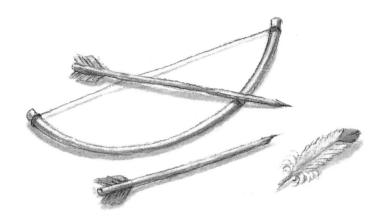

David ran to his usual hiding place—
under the old table. There was the book!
He quickly crawled in and started reading
about Little Crow.

"Your legs are sticking out. I can see
you!" called Sally. She spread a cloth over
the table.

"Shut up," growled David.

Sally always teased David when he was
reading. She was pretty old, thought
David, but she didn't understand a thing
about reading. And certainly not about
Indian adventure books.

"Little Crow, watch out for the bear!"
whispered David. Arrows flew
through the air around
Little Crow.

David couldn't put the book down. He was so deep in the story that he didn't notice Sally putting the birthday cake on the table. He didn't even notice the fine new fishing rod from Grandpa.

Granny stood in front of the tent and looked out at the woods.

"Where is Grandpa?"

"Here he comes now!" cried Sally, pointing at a dark figure in the distance.

Suddenly Granny stiffened.

Sally was scared. She wanted to scream, but Granny held her mouth closed and pulled her behind the tent.

Sally couldn't believe her eyes. A shaggy brown figure came right up to them and stood on its hind legs.

It was a bear!

He came straight to the table.

David was still underneath it, lost in his book.

Sally put her hands over her face.

"For heaven's sake, don't move, David," whispered Granny.

But David didn't hear.

The bear swiped at the birthday cake
and licked the sweet icing off his paw.
He did it again and again until he had
devoured the whole cake.

He stood up and sniffed to the left.
Then he sniffed to the right.

Granny held her breath.

The bear fell back on all fours, ambled down to the river, and swam across.

"The bear is gone!" cried Granny.

Sally ran to her brother and pulled him out from under the table.

"What's wrong?" asked David, surprised. Then he saw the birthday cake.

The tiny flags that had been stuck in the cake lay all over the place. A bit of cake stuck to the fishing rod.

"Sally!" cried David angrily. "You ate my cake!"

Just then Grandpa arrived. "Hey, did you see that bear over there?" he called.

"What bear?" asked David.

Sally showed Grandpa the birthday cake. "He got here before you did, Grandpa!" she said.

Grandpa was astonished. Then Sally and Granny told him what had happened.

"So reading is good for something," laughed Grandpa.

"It can even save your life," said Granny.

"David was lucky," said Sally. "Maybe he survived because it was his Birthday Bear!" She licked the last crumb of cake from the fishing rod.

"I'm as hungry as a bear," said Grandpa.
Everybody laughed.

Grandpa had brought a huge fish.
He handed it to David. "Here's a real
Blackfoot Indian birthday present," he
said. "We can roast it on an open fire."

"Oh, great! At least the bear didn't get
this!" cried David.

"Come on, Sally," Granny called. "We'll
make a new birthday cake."

Sally shrugged. "Okay, but let's eat it
right away before a bear gets it!"

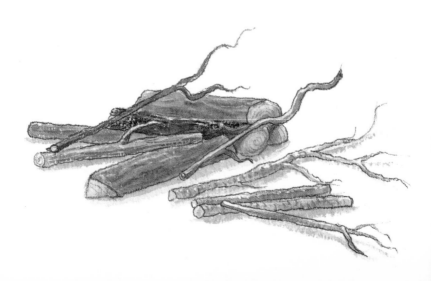

This is a true story. It happened almost exactly the way I've told it. And if you don't believe me, you'll have to go to the mountains yourself. But watch out—not all bears are birthday bears!

About the Author

Antonie Schneider was born in
Mindelheim, in southern Germany.
She has worked as an elementary-school
teacher, written a book of poetry, and
traveled widely. She lives with her
husband and three children in an old
house with a garden that has run wild—
with visitors, housework, books, and
stories (both true and imaginary).
She has written one other book for
North-South, *You Shall Be King!*

About the Illustrator

Uli Waas was born in Donauworth, Bavaria. She studied painting and graphics at the Academy of Graphic Arts in Munich. Since then she has illustrated many books for children, including three other easy-to-read books for North-South: *Where's Molly?*, *Spiny*, and *A Mouse in the House!* She lives with her husband, daughter, and son at the edge of the Swabian Alps.

About the Translator

J. Alison James was born in California. She makes her permanent home in Vermont, but recently spent a year in Norway. She studied languages and got a master's degree in Children's Literature so that she could write and translate books. She has written two novels and translated over thirty books for North-South.